8/17

LG 2.2 .5pt.

Ruby Rose

Off to School She Goes!

By Rob Sanders

Illustrated by
Debbie Ridpath Ohi

HARPER

An Imprint of HarperCollinsPublishers

www.harpercollinschildrens.com

ISBN 978-0-06-223569-5 (trade bdg.)

The artist used Adobe Photoshop to create the illustrations for this book.
Typography by Ellice M. Lee
16 17 18 19 20   SCP   10 9 8 7 6 5 4 3 2 1
❖
First Edition

To my students—past and present—
who inspire me to kick up my heels!
—Rob Sanders

For my eighth-grade teacher, David Smallwood,
who taught me how to dance
—Debbie Ridpath Ohi

When I heard I was going to start school,
I couldn't wait!

I wiggled my toes when I woke up.

I balleted during breakfast.

I belly danced while brushing my teeth.

Mom said that learning to sit still is a big part of school.

"Dancing is a big part of *me*!" I said.

When I got to school, I hip-hopped off the bus and bebopped down the hall to Ms. Dempsey's classroom.

"Hi. I'm Ruby Rose. I love to dance."

"Good to meet you, Ruby. I'm Ms. Dempsey.
I have never danced in my life."

"You should give it a try, Ms. D!" I said,
gliding to my desk.

"It's story time," Ms. D. said. "Everyone please
sit on the carpet."

"Let's cut a rug!" I cheered as I found a good spot.

"Let's sit quietly and listen," Ms. D. said with a smile.

So I sat quietly and listened.

Next, I arabesqued to art class and pirouetted to my easel.

"No dancing," Ms. D. said, a bit more firmly this time.

I pranced in P.E.

"No dancing," Coach objected.

And when I promenaded into the media center, the librarian whispered, "NO DANCING!"

"Time to line up for lunch," Ms. D. announced.

Step-heel, step-heel.

Brush.
Brush.

I tap-danced to the front of the line.

"Come on!" I said to my classmates.

Side shuffle.
Side shuffle.
Side shuffle.

Ms. D. raised her eyebrows.

Everyone stopped. But . . .

. . . I couldn't help it.

I leaped to my lunch table.

"No dancing," the lunch lady scolded.

I cancanned to the trash can.

"No dancing," the custodian insisted.

Everyone walked back to our classroom in a straight line.

"Time for a line dance!" I called.

Step. Step. And repeat.
Grapevine. Stomp. Clap! Clap! Clap!

Ms. D. held a finger to her lips.
Everyone stopped . . . *again*.

There was no dancing for the rest of the day.

No mambo during math.

No rumba during reading.

No samba during science.

At the end of the day, I raised my hand.

"Ms. D.?" I asked. "When do we dance?"

"I'm sorry, Ruby," Ms. D. answered. "There's no
time to dance at school."

"What?" I jumped to my feet. "No time to dance?"

The ant farm tumbled off the table, and thousands of ants scurried everywhere.

Ants crawled along the floor.
Ants squirmed into desks.
Ants crept up legs.

In no time, everyone was dancing!

The boys stomped and spun!
The girls whirled and twirled!

Even Ms. D. did the twist.
"See, Ms. D.! We *do* have
time to dance at school!"

Just as we finished cleaning up, the bell rang.

I hulaed down the hall and bounced onto the bus.

When I got home, I pranced into the house.

"I love my new school!" I told my mom as I skipped all the way to my room.

"Ms. D. is a great dancer!"

I poked my head back into the kitchen.
"By the way, Mom," I added, "we need
to buy Ms. D. a new ant farm."